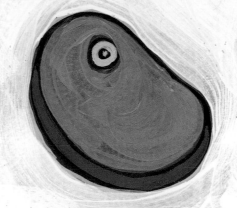

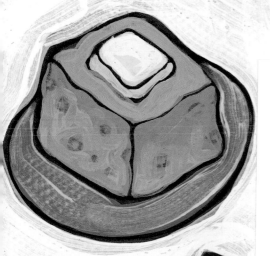

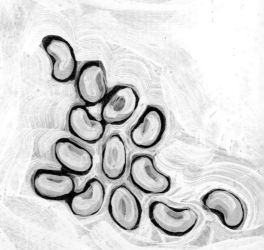

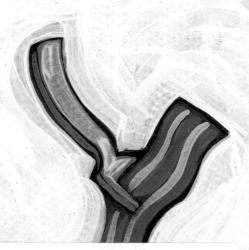

THE HIDDEN FEAST

A Folktale from the American South

Retold by Martha Hamilton & Mitch Weiss
Illustrated by Don Tate

AUGUST HOUSE
LittleFolk

LITTLE ROCK

Text copyright © 2006 by Martha Hamilton and Mitch Weiss
Illustrations copyright © 2006 by Don Tate

Published 2006 by August House LittleFolk,
P.O. Box 3223, Little Rock, Arkansas 72203
501-372-5450 http://www.augusthouse.com

Book design by Joy Freeman
Manufactured in Korea
10 9 8 7 6 5 4 3 2 1   HC

LIBRARY OF CONGRESS CATALOGING-IN-PUBLICATION DATA
Hamilton, Martha.
The hidden feast : a folktale from the American South / retold by
Martha Hamilton & Mitch Weiss ; illustrated by Don Tate.
       p.   cm.
Summary: The barnyard animals have a good time at their neighbors'
party until dinner is served, when the feast appears to be disappointing
and Rooster rudely storms off before discovering a hidden treat.
ISBN 0-87483-758-8 (alk. paper)
[1. Folklore—Southern States. 2. Domestic animals—Folklore.]
I. Weiss, Mitch, 1951- II. Tate, Don, ill. III. Title.
PZ8.1.H1535Hid 2006
398.2—dc22
                                    2005053101

The paper used in this publication meets the minimum requirements
of the American National Standards for Information Sciences—
Permanence of Paper for Printed Library Materials, ANSI.48–1984.

To the memory of Aunt Ruth Patrick,
who was sweeter than sweet potato pie, and
whose peach cobbler was good enough to die for.
—MH & MW

I thank God.
For Kolby—the best little art critic a dad could have. Thank you for liking
my pictures. Thank you for being honest when you don't like my pictures.
I look forward to sharing this book with you many bedtimes to come.
—DT

AUTHORS' NOTE:

Although this story's roots are African-American, it conjures up the best and worst about family get-togethers in any culture, from the food, the fun and games, to the relative who doesn't know how to behave properly. It brought to Martha's mind memories of her southern childhood with Sunday get-togethers at one of the aunts' or uncles' homes, games with dozens of cousins on the lawn, and food so good it made you want to "slap your pappy"! (It was always clear that "pappy" meant *stomach* because those who said it usually slapped their bellies as they spoke.) The oldest version can be found in *Nights with Uncle Remus* by Joel Chandler Harris (Boston: Houghton-Mifflin, 1883). More recent retellings are included in *The Last Tales of Uncle Remus* by Julius Lester (New York: Dial, 1994) and *One Hundred-and-One African American Read-Aloud Stories*, edited by Susan Kantor (New York: Black Dog and Leventhal, 1998).

This story contains several expressions, foods, and traditions that are characteristic of the culture of the southern United States and/or African Americans. For more information, consult the activity guide for this book at www. augusthouse.com.

—MH & MW

One day, the barnyard animals got an invitation. Their friends on the farm nearby were having a party.

The animals dressed in their Sunday best
and set off to see their neighbors.

Rooster led the way, strutting and crowing.

Duck waddled behind.

Cow moseyed along
in her own sweet time.

Pig strolled under his umbrella
to keep from getting a sunburn.

Goat pranced about, thinking of
the feast they were going to eat.

Horse trotted along, feeling fine.

Sheep made sure to keep in line.

Donkey walked right in the middle of the road,
    and Chicken crossed it
        to get to the other side.

The animals at the next farm knew how to throw a party. They had planned a whole afternoon of fun.

First they played Pin the Tail on the Donkey. Things did not get off to a good start, because Donkey did not want to play. But when Pig nearly pinned the tail on Duck, even Donkey had a good belly laugh.

Horse took off her shoes so that everyone
could play—you guessed it—Horseshoes.

When they played Hide-and-Seek,
Chicken was the hardest to find.

After the games, the animals sang and danced.

Pig broke out in a show of Hambone. The animals
hooted and hollered while Pig slapped himself silly.

Next, they sang a round of
"Old MacDonald Had a Farm."

Rooster made sure they all remembered their parts.

And what would a party be without the Hokey-Pokey?
The animals had a ball "shaking it all about."

When the dinner bell rang, the animals
scampered into the barn and sat down.

"Why, this is the prettiest sight
I've ever seen!" said Sheep.

"I can't wait to see what we have
for supper!" crowed Rooster.

The hosts brought in fancy bowls and placed them in front of the guests. But the only thing in each bowl was a piece of cornbread.

The animals were disappointed, but most of them were polite.

"My, it was nice of you to go to all this trouble,"
Horse said to the hosts.

"Bless your hearts for making such a fine feast,"
Cow added.

Pig could not wait to chow down.

"This cornbread makes me want to slap my pappy!"
he blurted out. "Let's eat!"

They all laughed. After Chicken said grace, the animals
picked up their forks—all except Rooster. He turned up
his beak in disgust.

"Cornbread! Is that all?
Why, I eat cornbread every day!"

With that, he turned and strutted home,
without a thank-you or a goodbye.

Donkey was embarrassed by Rooster's behavior.

"Don't mind Mr. Rooster," he told his hosts.
"He thinks he's the cat's meow."

The other animals dug into the cornbread.
Cow was the first to find the surprise.

"Laws!" she cried. "I just found some
mashed potatoes under here!"

"Look!" squealed Pig.
"Black-eyed peas, my favorite!"

But the feast wasn't finished.
Hidden under the vegetables the animals found dessert.

"Oh, my goodness!" hooted Horse.
"This chocolate pudding is divine!"

"Oh, my! Sweet potato pie
good enough to die for!"
squawked Duck.

"Peach cobbler!" bellowed Cow.
"I think I *have* died and gone to heaven."

Later, when the animals returned home,
they chattered on and on about the supper.

"That was the best meal I have ever had!"
Pig groaned with glee. He patted his stomach.

"You're right about that!" agreed Goat. "And who knew that
all those tasty treats would be hidden under that cornbread?"

When Rooster overheard all the talk, he was fit
to be tied. He could not believe he had walked
away from such a tasty meal.

But Rooster did not admit that he was wrong.
He never even apologized to his hosts for his
rude behavior. He just pouted in silence.

But since that time, Rooster has never
been fooled by what he sees on top.

Watch him in the barnyard when he finds a bit of food.
He scratches and scratches to get to the very bottom of it.
He wants to be certain that he will never miss another hidden feast.